DARK

BIBLE STORIES FOR ADULTS

W R Queensborough

"And the light shineth in the darkness; and the darkness comprehended it not." St John 1:5 KJV

DARK

BIBLE STORIES FOR ADULTS

W R Queensborough

Published by
QB Sound and Print

Copyright Information

DARK BIBLE STORIES FOR ADULTS

Author: W R Queensborough
Published by QB Sound and Print
Website address: www.qbsap.co.uk

ISBN 978-1-9162794-1-4

Also available as an eBook

Contents

Page	Title
7	Preface
9	Praise, Skin, and Bones
11	I Hear Weeping
13	Disrespected
17	Respite
19	Supremacy
21	Regrowth
25	I Remember
29	Your Secret Is Safe
33	Swoosh and Slice
35	Run!
37	Close…
39	My Firstborn
43	First Lady
45	him
47	Brother
51	The Offering

55 *Substitution*

57 *Returned*

59 *Sacrifice*

63 *Two Words*

67 *You Have Company*

69 *A Question of Suicide*

73 *Baby Food*

75 *These Foreigners*

81 *Sounds Like*

83 *Pursuit*

89 *Brotherly Love*

93 *I Saw You Last Night*

97 *Together Forever*

99 *It's A Split Decision*

107 *Men!*

109 *Withdrawn*

113 *It's Not The Fall, It's The Landing That Kills*

117 *For Crying Out Loud*

120 *About the Author*

121 *Books by the Author*

Preface

Lust. Murder. Betrayal.
Revenge. Justice. Redemption.

OKAY, SO WHEN I STARTED thinking about this collection of stories, there was a lot of talk about Game of Thrones (no spoilers)! Whatever you think about the graphic depictions, most would agree that it is a good story, packed with drama.

It prompted me to reflect that the Holy Bible is full of good stories and plenty of drama. They are also true stories, no matter how fantastical they sound, nor how sceptical the reader.

I retold one such story (*Respite*) and posted it on social media. A few friends commented how much they liked it, recognising the similar nature of the main protagonist with Arya Stark (again no spoilers!) So I put a few more out, and they liked those too, and asked for even more.

Inspired, I wrote more stories and here they are.

I have included scripture references so you can read the stories for yourself, and separate biblical facts from my creative imagination.

When I first decided I was doing this the original title was 101 Dark Bible Stories or something similar. Yeah, who was I kidding? There may well be another sixty or seventy stories there, but someone more creative will have to bring those out.

Can I tell you this? Some stories in this collection are dark. Horrific even. When I was a teenager, I remember reading one story (see *Returned*), then closing the Bible and deciding I would never read it again! The mindless savagery appalled me. There wasn't even an effort to justify what happened, well not in the story itself.

But the Bible does not exist to make everyone say 'ahh'. It exists to show us the mind of God, focusing on the identity and mission of Jesus Christ. The writers did this while painting an honest picture of humanity with all shades of life.

Lust. Murder. Betrayal.
Revenge. Justice. Redemption.

They are all in the Bible. And they are all right here.

W R Queensborough

Praise, Skin, and Bones

All glory belongs to God alone

THE KING FINISHED SPEAKING to thunderous applause. As he rose from his lavish throne, he took in the hundreds of courtesans present and lapped up their praises. His head turned from one side to the next as the crowd lifted their heads and hands and shouted his name. They likened his voice to the Great Almighty.

The king stretched out his arms and the roar threatened to take off the palace roof. He threw his head back to lap up more praise. A sharp biting sensation stabbed at his right hand, then his left. He looked at his right hand; nothing seemed wrong, but the pain increased.

As he looked at his left hand, bile rose into his mouth. Something moved under his skin. He followed the motion turning his hand over to see it move across his palm up to his wrist. At once his entire skin began to crawl from the inside. The skin on both hands became saggy as whatever was underneath consumed his flesh. He screamed for a full minute before the crowd realised.

The king's knees buckled. The skin on his forehead rose and fell at the same time that something sucked his cheeks inwards. His skull looked like a loose-fitting cloth covered it.

There was enough time for one more scream. Evidently whatever ate his flesh had left his vocal cords for the last.

*Adapted from Acts 12:21-24

I Hear Weeping

The heart of man is desperately wicked, but God is still in control

ANOTHER KING? THERE WAS NO room for another king. There was one royal line, one royal throne, and it was mine. Yet, these strangers stood before me, telling me a heavenly body had guided them here. Supposed birthplace of the King of the Jews.

I didn't know whether to take them as wise men or fools. I presume the former since they never returned to tell me if they found him. They must have seen what I was planning. My advisors told me stories from the ancient scrolls of one born in Bethlehem Ephrata who will rule with the rod of iron. Scrolls, stars, all foolishness. I alone rule in Judaea.

So I gave instructions to my soldiers. Kill every boy under two years old. They looked at me as if I must be mad. No, madness is allowing another to usurp my throne. So I told them again. Their faces questioned me one more time. I made sure they understood me.

Kill them all. Snatch them from cribs. Rip them from their mother's breasts. Whether eating, playing, or sleeping. Whether they are walking or crawling. Kill them all.

Sick ones. Healthy ones. Every colour, Jews and strangers. The happy ones and the crying ones. Fat ones. Malnourished ones. Spare none. There won't be much blood, they're only small. Kill them all.

Don't just go to Bethlehem. Go to Galilee, Jerusalem, Jericho, Capernaum, even Tyre and Sidon, go to them all. Every city, every village. Remember Ramah. From my palace, I want to listen to the mothers weeping in Ramah.

Check the highways and the hedges. Scan the rivers. And don't forget the bulrushes. We won't repeat that mistake.

Poor parents and rich ones. No bribes, no exceptions. Kill them all.

'Start with your own home', I told them. You can always have another child. If your fellow soldier hesitates, kill him. I can always get another soldier.

I am Herod, the only King of the Jews. Yes, it was me, I ordered the slaughter. Let history judge me how history wants, it doesn't matter – the message is the same.

Kill every single one. Kill them all.

*Adapted from Matthew 2:16-18

Disrespected

A vengeful heart is a terrible thing

UNCLE E, I HOPE YOU'RE OK. I'm sorry to bother you but I got to get this off my chest before I lose my mind.

The world has gone mad Uncle. 100 percent insane mad. Just to let you know, they raped our sister D. This prince wannabe from here in Shalem saw her in the field and raped her just like that. But uncle it gets worse. Now he says he loves her and wants to marry her!. Now get this. D says yes! What on earth??? Married, uncle. To her rapist. She's not even pregnant or nothing. What's that about? D's turned fool and making the whole family look fool.

Uncle, I'm not done there. Our dad agrees. No joke. My dad has said yes. So my sister has agreed to marry the man who raped her and my Dad has given his blessing. Reckons at least he's doing the honourable thing. Uncle, I know you and dad had beef back in the day. And I know you've kind of mellowed now. But can you believe this? I miss you, Uncle. You wouldn't have let anyone disrespect the family like this.

Uncle, I can't take it. And Sim is spitting fire. Our sister is a class girl from good breeding. We aren't like that. D's no whore, she could have married anyone she wants to, absolutely anyone. And this man disrespects her like that. The man's disrespecting all of us Uncle, you included.

If a man wants his thing, okay fine I get that, we're all men. But find a harlot, rough her up, take his thing from her. That's what she's paid for. Or go molest one of his own Shalem girls. Round here they probably used to that all day long. Just don't disrespect us, we're different class people.

But uncle me and Sim are working on a thing. By the time you pick up this message, it will be different. Remember how our people get circumcised, like great grandad taught us? Well me and Sim convinced Dad that if this guy wants our D he's got to do the same. Not only him, but the whole city. And it's not like they're babies, you get me uncle? These are big men, it will hurt.

I guess he must feel something for her if he's putting himself through all of that, him and his people. And D says she loves him. Maybe if things were different, it could have worked. But it's too late now. We have to do what we have to do. No one can let disrespect slide.

Uncle, you might not approve being as how you're changed. But these men will be hurting, and they will not recover. Serious. They're going to take a turn for the worse, you get me? When they've had it done, we will turn up and turn up.

Uncle, again I'm sorry to bother you with this but I just had to tell somebody. And at least if you hear anything you'll know the reason we did what we did. Dad was always the soft one, but I know you understand from back in the day. Say a prayer for me and Sim, Uncle. Things about to get dark.

Levi.

*Adapted from Genesis 34:1-31

Respite

Alluring, inviting, enticing…just don't turn your back.

SHE STOOD AT THE DOOR of her tent and begged him to hide inside. Tired, thirsty, and fleeing for his life how could he resist her?

Inside, he finished the milk that she had poured for him then lowered himself to the ground. Covering him over, she left him as he drifted off into a deep sleep.

She made no sound, left no footprint, as she returned moments later to his side and knelt beside him. Without hesitating, she hammered a tent peg through both of his temples, fastening his head to the ground.

*Adapted from Judges 4:17-21

Supremacy

Some you lose...

THE BATTLE BETWEEN THE BROTHERS escalated. They struggled to see in the darkness, but the vicious fight threatened to tear apart the same enclosure that had them trapped.

Each one knew they had to get out. They also knew that the best chance of survival would be to get out first. But each time one of them came close to breaking free the other hauled him back and so the struggle continued. The battle intensified, making the walls seem like they were closing.

Their mother watched them struggle, powerless to intervene. No amount of pleading or shouting drew either sons' attention long enough for her to reason with them. She was sure that if they only co-operated, they would both survive what waited ahead; neither one had to die. But on and on the war raged, and she felt each blow as only a mother could.

The older brother was born to fight, rough and ready from birth. The younger one fought to the end, but it was a losing battle. One last desperate lunge left him clutching his brother's heel. Somehow he clung on when his brother broke free, pulling himself to miraculous freedom.

The younger brother grew up knowing that if he was ever to contend with his twin brother, it would have to be with subtlety and guile. But subtlety and guile were his trademarks.

Their mother was just relieved that after nine months, the birth of the twins Esau and Jacob was over.

*Adapted from Genesis 25:21-28

Regrowth

It's never over until God says it's over

THREE TIMES HE HAD TEASED her about the source of his immense strength. And three times she had tried to deliver him to his arch enemies. Each time he had laughed it off, confident there was no danger. It was another chance to show off his great power and impress her again. He had fallen in love with her. He did not consider that she may not be in love with him. His adolescent ego could not imagine a woman who did not dote on him.

He was in her bed chamber again, his favourite place. But even he had noticed she was tiring of his games. It was fun for him but frustrating for her. Her frustration soon became his frustration. She pressed him daily for his secret, sucking the joy out of their time together. Before long, worn down by her continual nagging, he gave way, exposing his greatest secret. Her gratitude was immediate.

Relieved, he lay down with his head in her lap as she hummed and stroked his hair. Her lap, his hair, a soothing combination. Soon he rocked himself to sleep.

He awoke to shouting and realised the enemy was on him. As he stood up to brush them off another time something caught his attention. On the floor were his seven locks. He put his hand to his head and found nothing but bare skin. Someone had shaved his scalp clean, the source of his immense strength shorn. The enemy overpowered him while he was still in shock. He gave her a last look of disbelief as they dragged him outside.

The first thing they did was to put out his eyes. Then they set him to work grinding corn. He could go nowhere without being led. He ran his fingers over the ropes around his hands and feet. Mere days ago, he shredded the same ropes with a simple flex of his wrists. He bowed his head and let out a long low moan. He would have cried if he could.

When the Philistines threw their biggest ever celebration for all the lords and ladies, they led Samson out to be their source of entertainment. He heard the jeers, the mocking, the taunting as they paraded him around the arena like a helpless shackled beast. The worst though was the women. Their hands pawing at his body, their heavy breathing all over his face. Everyone of them sounded like Her, felt like Her. They even smelled like Her.

But the Philistines made one fatal mistake. In their merriment they never noticed his hair had started to grow back.

They were laughing when a young boy led Samson to the building's central pillars. They were still laughing when he cried out to God and started to strain against the pillars. When the first wisps of dust fell from the ceiling the laughing stopped. And when the first pieces of stone fell the running started. When the pillars and then the ceiling came crashing down, the screaming ended.

*Adapted from Judges 16:4-31

I Remember

Your sins have a way of catching up with you

AMNON HAD NOT SPOKEN WITH his half-brother Absalom in years. So the invitation to a family celebration took him by surprise. Why here, why now? The questions swirled as if caught up on gusts of fierce winds, Before he could wrestle for an answer to one, another assaulted his frontal lobe.

Still, as his father the king had asked him to go in his place, refusal was not an option. It would be a chance to meet up with others he had not seen in many years. True, they were never that close, but they were still brothers.

As he approached the great hall, the first hint of uncertainty caused Amnon's stomach to protest. The sight of his Absalom, host for the night, unnerved him. But he needn't have worried. Absalom's smile as he came to embrace him spread across the rugged face framed by those famed flowing rib length locks. His words put him further at ease.

"Come brother! It has been far too long since we have shared food and wine. We have many tales to catch up with. Of the men we have slain and the virgins we have bedded! Eat, drink, and be merry. Who knows about tomorrow?"

After four hours of mirth, the room rolled like a ship at sea. Drink after drink, story after story, Amnon's sides ached from too much laughter and much too much wine. He rose from his chair intending to relieve himself but collapsed instead. In a fit of laughter, he propped himself up on the floor.

"Now, kill him!"

In an instant a band of soldiers stood around him, knives drawn. The room hushed as Amnon looked around, noting the menace on their faces. He pointed at the one nearest before collapsing again laughing.

"Great," he shouted, clapping his hands. "Superb. You had me convinced."

He never felt the first half dozen stabs; the wine was a powerful anaesthetic. It was a slow process for the horror to creep up on him as the betrayal reached his mind. Even though dazed and confused, he still recognised Absalom as he came over and knelt beside him. In his dying moments he felt puffs of breath and soft lips on his left ear.

"Remember Tamar?"

It wasn't Amnon's whole life that flashed before him, it was one night, two years earlier. His eyes widened as he remembered what he had done to their sister. He reached up to his brother, coughing up blood.

"Jo-, Jo- …."

Absalom leaned in for his brother's dying confession, which constituted one word.

Amnon collapsed back into the dust, staring into nothingness with his eyes, while picturing Tamar in his mind. Despite all the wine he drank that night, he died sober.

*Adapted from 2 Samuel 13:1-29

Your Secret Is Safe

Wisdom and right will see you through in the end

SOMETHING WAS WRONG. WHEN a woman learns that she has been sentenced to be burned to death by her father-in-law, she does not remain seated as if nothing has happened. She runs, she screams, she tries to escape, or runs to her accuser and throws herself at his mercy. Anything at all to avoid the shameful execution that lies moments away

Instead, she looked up at the messenger from her couch, locking his face with hers. Maybe she hadn't understood him. Or perhaps she was in shock. Had the grief of losing her young husband all those years ago caught up with her? Had the fear of a painful death snapped her fragile mind?

Whatever was going on in her mind the messenger's eyes narrowed under a lined forehead, unable to hide his confusion. He could have sworn she was smiling.

*** ***

As the man passed by he noticed the woman sitting by the wayside waiting for trade. He couldn't explain the stirring. It had been many years since his wife passed away, yet he barely gave sex a moment's thought. And yet here he was, loins stirred, and about to pay a strange woman for her company and satisfy long forgotten desires.

As they engaged each other a nagging doubt tugged at him, wrestling with his lust. A guilt deeper than shame screamed this was wrong, desperately wrong. It screamed louder when he looked into her eyes. He saw a cold fire behind her pupils, irresistible and penetrating, inviting yet accusing.

The man screwed his own eyes shut and tried to divert his thoughts. The guilt rose with his increasing vigour until at last he let out a scream and pulled away. It was a moment of shameful satisfaction, his body shouting yes and his mind shouting no.

After returning to his own tent, he sent his servant to reclaim the personal items he had left behind for security. The woman was gone, as if she had never been. Rather than being angry, he breathed out and leant back.

*** ***

The messenger didn't hide his frustration, his scowl a clear sign that neither he nor his master were in the mood to be kept waiting. She rose from her cushion, slower than usual because of her recent weight gain. Instead of following the man however, she moved to the corner of her chamber and unravelled a folded cloth.

Turning back, she revealed a signet ring, two bracelets, and a wooden staff. She leaned forward, whispered in the servant's ear, then handed him the parcel. As he shuffled out of the room even more puzzled, she sat again on the cushion.

Judah paced the room until the messenger returned, without his daughter-in-law. Before he could react, the messenger handed the parcel to him. When he opened it, the hairs on his arm stood to attention, as he recognised his property. At that same moment back in her room, Tamar looked down and caressed her rounded stomach with both hands.

"It's going to be okay," she whispered. "It's going to be okay."

*Adapted from Genesis 38:1-26

Swoosh and Slice

Champions come in all shapes and sizes

THE BOY STOOD ON TOP of his world, having conquered his personal mountain. His baby cheeks flushed even redder than normal. His panting had nothing to do with exertion and effort, and everything to do with adrenaline rushing like wildfire through every fibre.

To the left of him, wild cheering and hugging from disbelievers trying to convince each other that what they were seeing in the valley below was real. To the right thousands more disbelievers standing motionless, hands over mouths seeking permission to gasp. Both sides held captive by a youth in a valley standing on a three-foot high mountain.

Women would make up songs about this day that would echo for years. Men would sacrifice their dying breath for him as his friend. Kings would offer him their daughters. If the boy expected any of this, he hadn't the slightest interest. He had done the necessary. No one else would, and no one else could. He alone was born for this.

The mountain beneath his feet moved as the chest of the giant heaved, gasping for an inrush of air. The boy stared down at the misshapen skull, forehead deformed by a crater that seeped blood mingled with brain matter. More blood oozed from giant ears, the corners of a giant mouth bearing red lines that trailed down giant cheeks.

The giant coughed, and the boy fought to keep his footing. The sling now cast aside, his pouch with the remaining four smooth stones swung from his waist. In his hands was the giant's own sword. As he hoisted it high over the giant's disfigured head an eerie hush descended on either side of the valley. All eyes fastened on the sword as it caught the sunlight. The boy's sinewy arms trembled under its weight.

Goliath's eyes, wild after the stone had crashed through his helmet, were now closed. David was unmoved. No room for pity. No space for mercy. Lion, bear, or nine-foot six-inch Philistine warrior, nothing can live that defies the Holy One.

The silence in the valley gave way to the sound of a swoosh and then a slice as metal met flesh and sinew. When metal meets flesh, even giant flesh, metal wins.

*Adapted from 1 Samuel 17: 49-51

Run!

When the Lord says it's time to get out, get out

THERE IS NO TIME TO WASTE, not even to gather their things. Everything they have longed for, fought for, and accumulated, they now have to leave behind. He had chosen this place to settle in for the lush prospects, ignoring the immorality. Now, they are mere moments away from destruction. It's about to rain fire and brimstone on the city, and they are still within the city limits. Some family members have refused to go. So be it. The four of them need to get out now or die.

The two deliverers grab them by the hands, two each, and by a miracle transports them to the edge of the city. They urge them to run and not look back. Even then they debate where they should head.

Destruction bursts behind them as the skies open over Sodom and Gomorrah. Father, mother, and two daughters running for their lives. They can feel the heat on their backs, taste the brimstone, ears deafened by the noise. The last thing they need to do now is to disobey their deliverers. The last thing they need to do is to look back.

Her steps become hesitant and she falls behind. Images form in her mind. The land, the home, the possessions. It was a good life in spite of the moral failings. And once their door was closed, did it really matter? Really?

Despite the warnings, despite the danger, Lot's wife looks back. Sure enough, it's the last thing she'll ever do.

*Adapted from Genesis 19:12-26

Close…

It doesn't hurt to be sure

THE COOL MOONLIGHT PERMEATED the tent walls, framing her unclothed silhouette. Even in limited light, she appeared more desirable than ever, something he never thought possible. Ever since he had first laid eyes on her, his mind had played out this scene so many times it was on permanent repeat. He had longed for this moment, when she would slide into his bed, and into his arms.

Now in the flesh every mental picture he had formed paled into insignificance. She walked over to where he was propped up and lay beside him. The brush of her body against his sent a tremor through his limbs. As he started to speak, a soft slender finger found and rested on his lips. Pressing on his shoulder, she invited him to lay back. As he reclined, he closed his eyes, waiting for her next touch. When the touch came, it did not disappoint.

It felt like hours must have passed before he dragged himself to his feet. After lighting a lamp, he returned. He shook his head and smiled as he gazed at her, tracing his fingertips up over her heels, ankles, calves. Everything sculpted to perfection, but larger than he had anticipated. He followed the same trajectory, up to the back of her knees, her thighs, and continued. He stroked her hair, before pulling on her shoulder and rolling her over.

He peered at her face, confused as he looked into her eyes. Soft and placid, there was no fire. Her eyes were missing the tension that first drew him. And they were the wrong colour. When the shekel dropped that this wasn't his beloved Rachel, but Rachel's sister Leah, Jacob's stomach heaved.

*Adapted from Genesis 29:16-18; 23-26

My Firstborn

Old Jamaican Proverb: if you can't hear, you will feel

I AROSE IN THE NIGHT, AWAKENED by an infernal scream, as if something had set the soul of every one of my ancestors on fire. The sound grew louder and louder until it came to the door of my chamber. As the door opened, I reached for my sword ready to despatch this foul spirit back to the realm of the dead.

The Queen entered, eyes and mouth wider than the desert itself, arms outstretched. She threw herself at me screaming 'he's dead, he's dead', punctuated by unearthly wailing. Then I heard the cries of the servants as if coming from the same obscene source.

A chill clutched at my chest, spreading throughout me. My head tightened. The room span, my knees gave way, but I stopped myself from falling to the ground. A loud voice boomed, then changed pitch to a screaming whine. 'The Prince? The Prince?' Over and over it repeated until I realised that the voice was mine.

When I reached his room, I was glad to see him sleeping. However, there were so many others in the room wailing I was sure they would disturb him. I ordered silence, and approached my son and held him, calling him to rouse from sleep. He ignored me, much to my displeasure, and when I loosed my hold, he flopped back onto the bed.

I screamed for the chief sorcerer to come forward and commanded him to wake the Prince. After minutes of incantations and applying a drink to his lips, there was no change. So I did what any Sovereign would do, I grabbed a sword from one of the palace guards and I skewered him, twisting the sword before removing it along with his bowels. Then I called for the rest of my sorcerers, ordering them to rouse the Prince. They too failed but time was too pressing for me to despatch them as well.

I embraced my firstborn again, pleading for a response. He lay in my arms with his head back, arms at his side, refusing to embrace me, or even acknowledge me. My son refused to breathe. I laid him down, walked to the window, and leaned on the balcony, head bowed.

The sound of a distant scream caught my ears. As I lifted my head, I noticed a lamp being lit. At that point, my eyes caught sight of something that still defies explanation, not by any knowledge known to any in my court. In the sky was something that looked like a cloud; not black, instead it swallowed light. The phenomenon was not moving as much as spreading, a thick lightless mass that enveloped the heavens. It had already passed over the place from where the scream originated. And as it seeped further across the sky more screams and lamplight filled the horizon.

I turned back towards the Prince but the Queen obstructed my view, glaring at me, accusing me. In other times I would have commanded the guards to insert hot pins into her eyes before slitting her throat. Yet she continued to accuse me with her silent gaze. I turned away and bowed to the ground with my hands over my ears. I could still see her face and hear the wail of the land of Egypt accusing me. By instinct, I recognised my crime.

I strode out of the Prince's chamber into my own and sent for Moses and Aaron. When they arrived my message to them was simple.

Go. All of you. Go.

*Adapted from Exodus 29:29-32

First Lady

God requires your faith; he does not require your help

MONTHS PASSED SINCE THE VOICE had spoken, but nothing had happened, no signs. She suspected from the outset it would be impossible. The moment she heard she laughed. And yet she allowed herself to come around to the idea. There was no doubt he believed, because he never gave up trying. She'd stopped enjoying love making long ago but as he spoke of little else, she tolerated it for his sake.

However, the pressure became unbearable. The worst part wasn't the physical effort; it was the hope. Hope that the miracle might be theirs, that promises can come true. This hope kept falling short. Then came the guilt. The feeling she was to blame. He would never say so, no he loved her too much. But she saw the truth in his eyes. Every time she asked him, he denied it, but she convinced herself anyway. She made her mind up; something drastic was needed.

At first, he took her suggestion to be a trick, a cruel test. Then he assumed she must be mad. But after a while, he agreed it might not be a bad idea. The girl was her servant after all, her property, so any child would still be hers and he would be the father, if he could ever manage such a thing. The servant was young, pretty if one likes long hair, pert breasts, and slender hips. If this was the only way, their sacrifice would be worthwhile. He reassured her he would think only of her, his beloved wife.

She had convinced him and given him her blessing. She even set the time. So why was she sick to the stomach? Why had she not eaten since? Why did she sense they were making a catastrophic mistake with far-reaching consequences?

And now, with him in there with the girl, why couldn't she rid her mind of the idea of them together? What possessed her to go to the tent, stand outside, and listen? She knew she might regret it, but she ignored the inner voice and pulled at the door. The sight alarmed her. There he was, this old man with a vigour remembered from days long gone.

As hard as that was, that's not what frightened her. Not even the face of her servant staring right back at her over his shoulder, peering into her soul and condemning her as worthless. No, that wasn't it.

It was when the servant girl smiled. Not the smile of a servant happy to please. It was the smile of a girl who knew that she had replaced her mistress and taken over. In her mind she had become the First Lady.

*Adapted from Genesis 16:1-4

him

Rejected? Don't worry, when they realise they need you, they will be back

THE ENEMY HAS BROKEN THROUGH your defences, intent on your destruction. They will rape your wives and your daughters and dismember your sons while they are still alive. Those are the fortunate ones. The ones not so fortunate will become slaves. They don't get to die once; they die every day. The enemy will burn your villages, fields, and livestock. And they will make you watch while they do this. That will be the last thing you will see.

Who will save you? Your king? There is no king. Who is coming to your rescue? Your generals? They ran off and are hiding. Your friend, your brother? They're just as scared and confused as you are. Who are you going to call? Don't know?

Well, I'll tell you. Call him. *Him?* Yes, that one, call him. *Are you sure?* Yes. The Outcast. The Harlot's Son. *Why him?* Because he knows how to fight. He's been fighting from boyhood. His brothers threw him out.

Rejected him because he wasn't pure stock. He was the Harlot's son; he didn't belong, didn't fit. Made the family look bad, so they threw him out and made sure he had no inheritance. Now he's leading others just like him. Rogues. Rejects. Outlaws.

Do whatever you need to do. Make him the leader if you have to, put him in charge of your army. If you want to live, you and your wives and children, there's no one else, no other choice.

What if he won't come? Oh, he'll come. He's been waiting for this moment ever since they threw him out.

Go ahead, call The Harlot's Son, That's right, him.

*Adapted from Judges 11:1-11

Brother

Vengeance has a long memory

As Abner sat by the well, he considered the command to return to the city. It was strange, given that his new king had sent him on a key mission, an opportunity to unite the entire nation, end the tribal infighting, and establish themselves as a major force. A deeper concern fuelled his hesitation. Joab.

If the call had come via anyone else, he would have already started his journey back. But with Joab in the picture only a fool would let his guard drop. After all it was Joab who had commanded the rival army when they fought on opposite sides. Joab whose army won the day and caused him to run for his life. And it was Joab's younger brother who pursued him afterwards.

*** ***

Abner held no quarrel with Asahel; he was a just youth, a runner not a fighter like his elder brother. But he would not give up the chase. Running across plains, sliding down steep inclines, scrambling over rocks. The terrain took its toll on Abner, meanwhile Asahel just kept on coming.

More than once Abner had warned him to give it up or else. Impetuous to the end, Asahel left Abner no choice; he had to stop him.

The experienced fighter spotted a rock ahead of him and flipped his spear around in his hand. He let his pursuer get within three paces, then planted the spear end at the base of the rock and came to an abrupt stop. He didn't even look back as Asahel ran straight onto the spear.

When Abner turned around he saw the spear had penetrated Asahel's slim body and came out through his back. Abner watched the blood trickle from the corner of the young man's mouth even as the light faded from his eyes.

*** ***

The last time Abner spoke to Joab he reasoned that pursuing this private war made no sense. To his relief, Joab agreed; to kill Asahel was easy. Killing Joab, a seasoned warrior, was a tougher proposition.

Has he given up the feud, or is he still out for vengeance? Abner convinced himself that the king would never allow Joab to threaten the peace, and the opportunity to strengthen his armies, over a personal feud. The king was one to look beyond petty matters. Even when fighting on opposite sides he had marvelled at how the king had shown great restraint when he had chances to destroy his own enemy.

Keen to show his pledged allegiance to the king he rose, saddled his horse and started back.

As he drew near to the city gates, it was Joab who greeted him. Doubts rose again, and his arm twitched as he fought the impulse to reach for his sword. But he reasoned that respect and honour for great rivalry would keep him safe. Not to mention having the king's protection now he had changed sides.

The former enemies embraced. Relief eased the tension in Abner's muscles. The past was the past, rivalries abandoned, a glorious future awaited as two mighty warriors stood side by side.

"For Asahel", whispered Joab.

Cold metal pierced warm flesh, driving up and through into Abner's lungs which began to gurgle as a baby. Blood spewed over his adversary's shoulder. In the four seconds he took to die, Abner realised that with Joab, family honour was never petty.

*Adapted from 2 Samuel 2:17-28; 3:21-27

The Offering

The effects of abuse are far-reaching; don't suffer in silence

SITTING NEXT TO EACH OTHER, backs to the wall of the cave, the sisters stared at him without saying a word. The connection they had needed no words. As children they were like any other sisters - play, fight, make up, play.

But since the day of the offering everything had changed. What they heard that night united their hearts in an unholy fear. That night they hugged each other and wept into the early hours. When he threatened beatings, they screamed louder and held each other tighter. No one would ever take either from the other. Their mother found them asleep in each other's arms, inseparable.

From that night on, a bond born out of emotional trauma knitted their spirits and minds in an unbreakable tie. Now they shared one another's physical pain, each one knowing by instinct when the other was hurting. Sometimes they finished each other's sentences, ate the same food, sometimes from the same plate.

As they sat side by side watching him, each one replayed the moment their lives changed forever; the night two sisters became an offering. The night two strangers turned up at their dwelling whom their father invited to stay. They relived the sounds of the mob that swarmed their house, baying for fresh meat to satisfy base sexual urges. Terrified, they remembered him stepping outside and pleading not to harm his guests. They listened as he, that man, bargained to save his new friends.

'Take my daughters instead. They are virgins. Do what you want.'

Take my daughters instead. Do what you want. Take my daughters instead, do what you want. The words were burned into their psyche.

The younger sister still wept for her mother. She never escaped that cursed place because he refused to go back for her. He abandoned her, disposed of her to save his own skin.

The older sister was more pragmatic. She had learned on those two occasions a hard lesson that became her mantra. You do what you have to do. Even if it means sacrificing others. Daughters, wives, makes no difference. You do what you have to do.

She turned to her younger sister.

"Remember how we always wanted to have children." Her sister nodded.

"And you know there are no men around here in this forsaken place." Again her younger sister nodded in agreement.

"No other men."

The word 'other' took a while to register. But when the younger sister caught up, she turned to look at him. Disgust rose, not at the suggestion, but at him. What he had done to them, to their mother. She turned back and stared into her sister's eyes.

Without words, she got up, fetched wine and brought it to her sister, and they both approached him. They knew how much wine they needed to get him drunk enough, they'd seen it often. When he got there, the younger sister took a step backwards.

"Are you sure about this?" she asked.

Her older sister positioned herself over her father, adjusted his robe as well as her own, then turned to her.

"You do what you have to do."

*Adapted from Genesis 19:1-8: 30-36

The Substitute

Darkness lurks in more than one place

AS THE WICKED ONES CIRCLED his house, the Master knew what they wanted. Their reputation was no secret.

Whenever they sensed fresh victims, their depravity sunk lower. So it was no surprise when they demanded he sends out his visitor. His visitor, a holy man, was no stranger himself to the ways of evil perversions that lay within men's hearts.

The Master of the House shouted from the rooftop, trying to appease the men assembled at his gate. He offered a simple proposition - take his virgin daughter and his guest's lover instead. The Wicked Ones were hell-bent on sampling their own gender. Why settle for commonplace girls when there was a man, a stranger, ripe for picking? The red lust had descended.

The priest recognised these men with dark hearts and depraved lusts. Throw a large bone to a ravenous beast, and he is unlikely to hold out for steak. Taking matters into his own hands, he pushed his lover out through a hidden door. Back inside he informed the Master who directed them to her.

The priest's lover tried to scream but nothing came out. She beat on the door with hands that soon became bloodied. By the time she turned around, up to a dozen men had surrounded her. She found her scream. The Wicked Ones eyed their prey, baying silenced. They saved their strength for something else before the night ended.

*Adapted from Judges 19:14-25

Returned

Without godly law, darkness intensifies

AS THE PRIEST TRIED TO LEAVE his host's residence, he stumbled over the package returned to him on the doorstep. At his feet lay a bundle of torn bloody rags that was his lover. The trail in the dust showed how she must have dragged herself the last part of the journey back to a familiar territory.

The priest pictured her journey, pictured every act of degradation, every torturous abuse she must have endured through the night. His vision went beyond her body as he peered into her wounded soul, her crushed spirit. Several times he called to her, with not so much as a groan in response.

He picked her up from the threshold, placed her on his donkey and returned home. Once inside, he placed her on a low wooden table. He stared at the broken mess that had been his companion on so much of his own journey. What he saw was the depravity of mankind left to their own unrestrained base lusts.

His response had to send a message for the nation that they would remember. A message warning of the depths of wickedness found only when people dwell in darkness. It had to be a message that addressed the savagery of a fallen destitute people, so lost that even holy men took concubines.

As he reached for a knife, he stared once more at his near-dead lover, then with precision he dismembered her body. Twelve pieces, one for each tribe, dispatched to the length and breadth of the land. And so, the priest testified of what happens when there was no rule in the land.

*Adapted from Judges 19:1, 25-30

Sacrifice

Serving means sacrifice

THE PRIESTS STOOD ARRAYED IN their priestly garments, heads held high, surrounded by the king's soldiers. The soldiers had assembled the priests without force, none had resisted. Their hearts were heavy, but not for themselves. They had always known ever since they answered the call to the priesthood, that they could not offer a sacrifice without being prepared to be a sacrifice.

Their heaviness was for their nation. A chosen people and a proud nation that had overcome despots, years of bondage, a red sea, hunger, thirst. They had survived armies, crossed uncrossable rivers. They had called on their God and defeated their enemies. Yet now, a chosen people were being destroyed from inside. Destroyed by the one set up to lead them, to reign over them. A madman, designated as king, plagued by evil spirits. Tormented by the success of others raised up to deliver them.

But though their hearts were heavy, their heads did not bow. They stood holding their heads looking up to the hills, seeking divine help. They refused to look at their inquisitor. Their king.

"Which one of you is for my enemy? Which one of you feeds him and shelters him? Who of you places weapons in his hand and sends him to commit treason against the Lord's anointed?"

Silence.

"Which of you is for your enemy, and against your king?"

Ahimelech, chief of the priests, lowered his eyes and looked at the king.

"My Lord, we are the servants of The Most High, the God of our fathers Abraham, Isaac and Jacob. We are neither against our king nor for him who you name your enemy."

"You have given him the bread of priests. You have handed him the sword of the Philistine. When he comes for your king, he comes because of you. Do you deny this?" The chief of priests raised his chin and looked back up to the hills.

"Soldiers bear arms!" The company of soldiers drew their swords and took their stance.

"Fall on your king's enemies! Slay them. Spare not any."

The soldiers looked at the priests, then at each other, then turned to their commander. He surveyed the company of priests, holy men of the Holy One. Duty warred with conscience for indeterminable moments, before he sheathed his sword and stood to attention.

Every soldier did the same. The king tore his outer garment and cursed an oath.

"Will no one fight for the Lion of Israel? Will no one defend the King? So be it. Come, Faithful One."

From the shadows The Edomite stepped forward, dagger drawn. The former chief of the king's herdsmen, The Edomite had nurtured plans for a position of influence greater than anyone had realised. As a master of stealth, he had risen to a position amongst the king's personal guard by doing what others feared to do. His whispers had sentenced many to death at the mouth of the king, all accomplished from the shadows. Today he stepped into the public light.

He approached Ahimelech and stood face to face with him. The chief priest looked back at him then closed his eyes. The Edomite sneered. A herdsman of his experience had slaughtered countless animals. A priest, even one as notable as Ahimelech, would be a small step up.

He lifted his dagger and drew a thin red line across Ahimelech the priest's throat, stepping back as he collapsed to the ground. He stepped over his body and moved to the nearest priest and stared into his eyes. The priest stared back, then closed his eyes, and lifted his head exposing his throat. The Edomite obliged.

Eighty-five priests in total. Bodies upon bodies. Blood mingled with blood. And underneath their armour, soldiers wept.

*Adapted from 1 Samuel 22:8-18

Two Words

Know your self-worth, even when others don't

THE CELEBRATION WAS AT ITS height when the message for the Queen arrived. Royal women from kingdoms near and far had gathered around her, while the King entertained his royal guests elsewhere. The Queen betrayed no emotions as she rose and went towards the exit.

One last glance. One last sweep of the hall. Laughter. Not the forced kind meant to appease vain men who thought themselves funny. Genuine, rib-tickling, good-natured, unrestrained laughter coming from esteemed women with no pressure. Stories being swapped of triumph and sorrow, and the ridiculous nature of the male ego. Stories of love and heartache shared amongst kindred spirits.

As the Queen entered her chamber accompanied by her trusted maidens, her mask faded. The call from the King could only mean one thing. It was time for the exhibition, for her to parade naked in front of drunken loutish boys in kings' clothing. Time for the men to leer, point at, and lust after her, an object of gross fantasy. All for the satisfaction and pride of her husband the King, himself by now overtaken by wine and lowered to the place of common boors.

The seven messengers at the door implored haste, wary of the threat to their own lives should they stretch the King's impatience beyond limit; he was eager to display his envied treasure. The Queen's attendants urged their Majesty, knowing full well the King's pride, yet feeling her heaviness.

The Queen stared at her reflection and saw again who she really was. She was not her crown and jewels and fine clothes and riches. She was not her body, sculpted by her Maker and pampered by her maids to be the envy of kings and queens. In her reflection she recognised her true self and settled in her heart whatever happened next no longer mattered.

Queen Vashti gave her maidens a message to take back via the King's messengers to His Highness himself. As the door closed, she settled herself on her couch and waited. She knew that the next time her door opened, her story would reach the final chapter. Her eyes closed, and she smiled as a cloud of serenity descended.

The King saw the chief of his messengers hesitating and could not contain his irritation. He signalled for the messenger to come with haste. The messenger approached and his forehead scraped the floor, so low was his bow. He arose, then bowed again to the King's ear. The King let the words sink in past his hearing. A fire kindled on his skin even as a bolt of lightning shocked his heart. The message shrieked in his skull, threatening to cleave his head open, reverberating louder and louder.

The Queen had only sent him two words.

“Not tonight.”

*Adapted from Esther 1:1-12

You Have Company

Stop trying to impress others

"NO MORE! PLEASE MAKE IT STOP."

"No one said you had to give all of the money."

"But that's what everyone else did."

"That was up to them. You didn't need to."

"We would have been the odd ones out."

"We?"

"I. I mean I would have stood out. And who said the rest of them gave the apostles everything they sold their houses for?"

"You don't see any of them here do you?"

"Oh my Lord! Help me!"

"Hot?"

"Unbearable! How come this heat doesn't affect you?"

"I'm a guard, not a resident."

"It's not fair. Not fair!"

"No one else to blame."

"Hope my wife is ok. She doesn't deserve this."

"Did she agree with you?"

"Well, yes, but the idea was mine. She just followed my lead."

"Ok."

"Please tell me she will be ok."

"Depends on what she says when she gets to the meeting."

"You mean, there's a chance she might end up here too?"

"If she tells the truth she'll be fine. If she follows your line, it's not looking good. Her choice."

"No. Please. Warn her before it's too late. She couldn't bear this. Please tell me she'll be ok."

"Erm.... about that..."

"What? What?"

"The meeting has just broken up."

"And?"

"And it looks like you'll be having company."

"No! No! Please no!"

*Adapted from Acts 5:1-11

A Question of Suicide

No need to fret over those who betray you; their day is coming

"BAILEY? YOU IN HERE?" Detective John Scotland poked his head around the door.

"Over here sir."

Scotland entered, nodded in Bailey's direction, then glanced around the room. "Ok so what we got?"

"Looks like an obvious suicide."

Scotland scanned the room again before responding. "What makes you think that?"

"He was found hanging right up here sir." Scotland stepped back to get a better view. Bailey continued.

"Door was locked from the inside. Everything in it's proper place apart from this overturned table. No sign of struggle or forced entry."

"Who found the body?"

Bailey flicked through his notes. "One of the servants sir. Maid tried to get in to clean the room. She had to get someone to break the door down."

"Ok. Do we know the victim's name?"

"Ahithophel, sir. A royal counsellor."

"Ahithophel. Wait. Isn't he the one who switched sides? Started working for the King's son, against the King?"

"Yes sir, that's him. They say listening to him was like listening to the voice of God himself."

"Is that so? So, what would make him want to take his own life?"

Bailey tipped his Trilby back and scratched his head. "Word on the street says the king's son ignored his advice. Started listening to another counsellor. Younger. I guess he felt as if he had lost his edge."

"Come on Bailey. You reckon that was enough for him to take his own life? A guy like him with everything he's got going for him?"

"Well sir, someone of his standing prides himself on being the absolute top dog, voice of God as it were. Pretty hard to take when someone else has taken his place. Guess he just couldn't live with that. Pity."

"Sure is, Bailey, sure is. Ok, I think we're done here. Might as well leave the boys to collect any evidence. Oh, did he have any family?"

"I believe he was grandfather to Bathsheba."

"Bathsheba? Queen Bathsheba? Wait, wasn't she Uriah's wife? You mean, that Bathsheba?"

"That's the one sir."

Detective Scotland rubbed his stubbled chin. "Mmm, I see."

*Adapted from 2 Samuel 15:12 & 31-34; 16:21-23; 17:1-23. See also 2 Samuel 11:3,4,14,15. Oh, and almost every detective show in the whole wide world.

Baby Food

You think it's unthinkable?
Well think again!

"I DEMAND JUSTICE O KING."

The king had become wearied by the constant disputes coming before him. He had to settle petty arguments while matters of a far more serious nature threatened his kingdom. The famine that gripped the land had created devastation. Soon they would have to bow to their enemy who laid siege as a python constricts its prey.

"Plead my cause O Lord!"

The king looked at the woman standing with her petty complaint. How could it be fitting for a man of his stature and majesty to deal with the trifling matters of lowly peasants? Despite his annoyance, he gave this loud one permission to speak.

"My Lord, on account of the great famine that has pressed us, I agreed a plan of action with another woman. O King we understand that such matters do not concern palaces. But we, your people, are being laid waste.

"We have both given birth to babies just days old. With great anguish, we agreed to eat my baby yesterday and her baby today. Well, yesterday we boiled and feasted on my baby. Today, she has hidden hers I know not where."

The king tore his clothes, then sank to his knees, clutching his head.

"O king, demand of her the child. I need to eat!"

*Adapted from 2 Kings 6:26-30

These Foreigners

To stupid people racism makes sense

"THERE'S NO OTHER WAY to say this, but: our nation is at crisis point. These immigrants are over here taking over our country. And what does our great leader do? Puts them in positions of power. It's an utter disgrace. How can they be allowed to rule over us? They don't respect our laws or our customs, they follow their own ways. They refuse to fit in, then try to tell us how we should live our lives? These people walk around so full of themselves, as if they're superior, talking in their own language and sticking to themselves.

"We should never have allowed so many of them to come. Why didn't we leave them where they were? They're not our responsibility. It's nothing to do with us the fact that their own leaders were so corrupt.

"Listen, my stance is nothing to do with race, I've never been a racist. But we can't escape basic facts. They're slaves, nothing more, never will be, just look at their history. You can't put them in charge. They're not intelligent, they can't even manage their own affairs. You'll never change them. The sooner we get rid the better. The big three are making a mockery of our great nation. If we remove them, the rest will fall into line."

Even by Kuri's standards, this latest rant was epic. Long known for his hatred of all things foreign, Kuri longed for the complete destruction of everything that did not fit with his version of patriotism. From the noise in the room, he was far from being alone.

"We need patience."

The room erupted. The last thing they wanted to listen to was Shamash trying to reason. Everyone regarded him as a weak-willed liberal politician who had nothing to contribute in these times of national crisis. In times past his position as an elder statesman guaranteed him respect from people many years his junior. He had seen times of success and of struggle and appreciated their history in a way few could match.

But times and ideas had changed, leaving him at odds with the mood of people with no mind for peace and tolerance. This was a time for thugs in nice clothes to revel in public tirades and in private brutality. Xenophobia was the order of the day. Despite the objections, Shamash continued.

"We cannot launch ourselves into actions that will further tear our nation apart. These people are here now.

They are an integral part of our nation, with rights as others."

The room sparked again into an uproar. Balthazar stood up and motioned for silence. The room quietened.

"Please, let us keep order. We are not common folk. Allow Shamash to finish."

Shamash eyed Balthazar. Wisdom taught him not to fear the rabble rousing Kuris of this world. Loud and ignorant, men like him were commonplace. Shamash knew that it was the Balthazars that posed the greatest threat. Skilled orators in public, ruthless manipulators in private. If Balthazar was allowing him to speak it was only because it was to his own personal gain. He resumed his speech.

"The wisdom of the so called big three, along with their mentor, is hard to resist. They have proven themselves over and again as people with insight and foresight. The way they carry out their roles is plain to see. Their advice has helped show order, and given the king much needed direction, helping to keep our nation as the world power.

"Consider what they endured. Carted away as children from their nation and brought into a foreign land. Yet they have not only survived, they have thrived. As for their lack of intelligence, see how easily they learned our language and converse in the palace. I wonder, how many of us can speak theirs?

"They have not acted to discredit or weaken our nation, they have helped to improve our standing in the world through their service."

The voices of dissent roared their disapproval before once again being silenced by the masterful Balthazar.

"Thank you Shamash for your words. It is always an honour to listen to you; your vast experience deserves as much. This gathering recognises your great service to our nation over a long and distinguished career.

"If I may, I wish to address a point you made. You were correct to identify their great wisdom and impact upon our nation. Only a fool can view them as lacking intelligence."

Kuri's face flushed as Balthazar continued.

"However my dear friend, those facts present the greatest threat to our great nation. The king is now under direct foreign influence. If we do not deal with these people, and leave them unchecked, what is to stop them from turning the king's head, and leading us to a place where we surrender all national pride? What if they recommend peace and negotiation instead of conquest? Conquest has been our way and has made us the greatest power in the world. Should we abandon our way, our history, our culture, on the say so of people foreign to us?

"Should we let this continue, how will our nation look in twenty years' time? How will your grandchildren fare when they in effect become the ethnic minority? Did our forefathers sacrifice their lives, shed their blood, so that the empire they fought for becomes an annexe of foreign states?

"It is time to remove our enemies from power and put them back into the fields. Those who refuse we must view as traitors. And we know the penalty for treason."

Shouts of approval reverberated around the room. Shamash recognised that his lone voice held no sway. He resigned himself to defeat.

"I say we put an end to this," Kuri shouted. "Rise, kill them!"

Kuri stirred their hate as he thumped the table. Once again it took Balthazar to bring calm. His hatred of things foreign exceeded Kuri's, but it carried a sophistication that made it a darker threat than any bluster Kuri could muster.

"There is no need for us to lift a finger against these men; they will destroy themselves."

Balthazar's words gripped the gathering. He revelled in having them in the palm of his scheming hands.

"Yes, they will destroy themselves. A decree went out commanding our entire nation to bow and worship the king's new statue when the minstrels play the chosen music. And defiance of the king's command is punishable by death in a fiery furnace.

"I have evidence that these three men refuse to bow when commanded. I understand these men. They hold to a strange god named Yahweh-Elohim, who forbids them to worship any other god, or graven images.

"This evening I will bring the evidence before the king. Our king is intemperate, he will not allow such defiance. He will command them again to bow and worship, and without doubt they will once more refuse.

"Why soil our own hands when our king himself will carry out the task for us?"

Shouts of affirmation once again shook the walls. Hands banged on the table, as feet stamped on the floor. Kuri quietened the room enough to make one more point.

"Balthazar, I ask one thing. When the time for execution comes, I want to be there. I want to hear them scream with my own ears."

"Kuri, I will recommend you have the honour of throwing them into the furnace yourself."

The room erupted.

*Adapted from Daniel 3:1-30

Sounds Like

Some poor decisions have a way to haunt you.

"MAKE IT STOP. MAKE IT STOP!"

The king fell to his knees, again covering his ears. His cries of anguish resonated throughout the entire palace, causing all the servants to quake. When he was like this, everyone was at risk, be it stable lad, armour bearer or chief advisor.

"Can't you hear it? Can't you hear it?"

The royal attendants knew better than to respond. It was enough they appeared near enough to help. The smart ones were distant enough to escape.

"Make it stop. Please, make it stop!"

He tried but did not drown out the noise with his own screaming and sobbing. It was another three parts of an hour before his torture eased. During that time a spear impaled one servant, another had his right hand all but severed.

The advisors consulted yet again. No one could imagine what hellish sounds the king endured, never mind how to combat it. They concluded that there must be unknown evil forces at work, causing him torment for some inexplicable reason. Maybe something he had done. Something in his past that demons were replaying back to him. It was a new advisor who came up with a simple plan.

"Give him something else to listen to. Drive out the noise in his head with something melodious. I know of a man with eight sons. The youngest son is skilful with music, gifted by The Most High."

As one they agreed. They would have agreed to anything they had not tried before. They brought the young lad to the king, and every time the king suffered the lad's playing calmed his spirit. The bravery of the lad became legendary.

On one particular occasion, the king suffered yet another attack, worse than anything so far. Rather than distance himself the young lad came closer than ever before but this time refused to play. The servants were beside themselves, fearing that the king would tear down the palace with his bare hands, stone by stone. Yet the lad would not play. Instead, he shouted at the king.

"What do you hear?"

"Make it stop! Make it stop!"

"What do you hear? Tell me!"

"Make it stop! Or. I. Will. Kill. You."

"No! Tell me what do you hear? Now! Tell me! Now!"

"The sheep! The sheep! The bleating of the sheep!"

The lad gripped his harp, again releasing sounds that only angels could have orchestrated. For a season at least, the bleating stopped.

*Adapted from 1 Samuel 15:7-15; 16:14-19

Pursuit

It's hard not to end up lost with the crowd

WHEN THE SUPERNATURAL CLOUD finally lifted, Bak led the pursuit from the front. He drove his chariot with the fury of ocean waves. His eyes focused ahead on the quarry, but his thoughts were elsewhere, back in the past.

On that unforgettable night they were still awake at midnight. The week-old baby Baky suckled on Nefertiti as she reclined on the couch. Bak looked on, heart melting with pride and gratitude. This was not a task to pass to her maid, not after waiting twelve years for their first child. Not after years of weeping, sacrifices to the gods, and continual disappointment. The reproach of her adversaries had worn her down to a point almost beyond despair. But looking now at Baky's rosy cheeks and hearing him gurgle, every pain disappeared.

Bak watched Nefertiti switch her gaze from him to Baky and back again. He loved remarking on his son's resemblance to him, teasing her that maybe the next one will at least have her nose.

His keen ears picked up the sounds of screams in the distance, his soldier's instinct moving him to the window. Bak watched as a thick cloud he couldn't describe spread, yet roll itself over the sky towards them and connected it to the cries. As he watched the cloud spread overhead, the next scream came from behind him. Spinning around, his heart clutched at his throat.

A thick mass that swallowed light lifted from the couch where his wife and son were laying. It moved and shifted towards him, momentarily taking on the form of a man, then to a shapeless cloud. In the brief moment that it enveloped him, time stood still. No sight, no sensation, no sound. It was as if everything in the world had ceased to exist.

When the room reappeared he sprang towards the frantic Nefertiti who was clutching Baky and throwing herself forward and backwards. The screams turned to wailing, mangling his insides. All he could do was embrace them both and release his own wails.

Bak reverted to his physical eyes and the present, set his jaw as a rock, and urged his horses even faster.

To the extreme right flank young Ptahhotep struggled to focus as his chariot trundled forward. A mere six feet away stood an impossible wall of water scaling so high he could not discern the top. Ptahhotep had gathered since the first of the ten national disasters that something above nature was at work. He knew that the power of the gods he worshipped growing up did not compare to this unknown god, a being far beyond comprehension.

The water behind the invisible wall churned. Ptahhotep feared the wall must at any second collapse and sweep him away to the underworld. A large fish swam to the wall's face and Ptahhotep's mouth gaped open as his bowels emptied. The fear transmitted to his horses, both of whom reared up, sending his chariot into the chariot next to him and unseating the rider. Ptahhotep turned and saw the rider crash to the ground, and become entangled under the hooves and wheels that had been following hard behind. He cried out to his subordinate gods, begging to go back home. The water beside him and the thousands of chariots at his back meant there was no way to end this charge into oblivion. He and his chariot continued at breakneck speed.

It was Khahor's sense of duty that carried him forwards right in the middle of the pursuing host. A veteran of many campaigns, faithfulness had been the mantra that sustained him. He was the third of his generation of the military might of Egypt and expected another three of his future generations to do the same.

And yet Khahor knew that no matter the outcome, he had changed forever. He had engaged with the slaves, and with one in particular. Hadar served his wife from she was a child, growing up more a daughter than a slave; the child that his wife had longed to have. After his wife had died Hadar continued serving in the household. Through her Khahor had looked beyond the surface, and had taken time to understand their history, their culture, their worship. Hadar taught him the story of Abraham leaving Ur to go to Canaan. Of Isaac and Rebekah. Of the struggle in the womb of Jacob and Esau, of Joseph's trials and eventual promotion to the second most powerful man in Egypt.

Khahor had known well before the first plague that those named gods were of his own people's invention. There was only one true God. El-Shaddai, El-Elyon, many names but only one God.

Khahor was fascinated by the story and captivated by Hadar. His feelings had evolved. She had crossed over in his desire from servant to something much more intimate. Duty carried him forward, where truth and love would have turned him around.

The pursuing army crossed the mid-point of the sea drawing ever nearer to their prey but then, calamity. One by one chariot wheels became detached from axles, crippling the army. Khahor was catapulted from his chariot onto the loose wheel of another chariot, instantly breaking his back. Ptahhotep fell to the ground screaming as his sanity at last departed. In his madness he confessed what he had long suspected; this unknown god was unlike any other.

Bak had been out in front leading the chase when his chariot crashed. His horses bolted leaving him stranded. He was near enough to see the last of the slaves cross to the other side. As he closed his eyes in frustration, he pictured Nefertiti cradling Baky. Their only son, their firstborn. Her wails pierced his ears again, searching after his soul. He felt a pain tear his chest in two which drove him to his knees. He threw his head back and released his own shriek of anguish. When he opened his eyes, he picked up his bow and started to run towards the slaves, fuelled by bloodlust. It was impossible, yet he got closed the distance.

Close enough to recognise the familiar shape of a man standing with hands outstretched. The same man who had returned from forty years on the run, and now had killed his firstborn. Bak could not understand why the Pharoah had not put him to death the moment he came back.

Tears stung Bak's eyes as he stared at the fugitive who forty years ago had murdered his grandfather before escaping into the wilderness. He attached an arrow mid-stride and pulled back his string just as the walls of waters broke.

Bak, Ptahhotep, and Khahor, all in pursuit of the children of Israel. Three individuals, each with their own motivation. But when Moses stretched out his hands that second time, hate, fear and duty clung to each other in death. The waters returned, burying Bak, Ptahhotep, Khahor together.

*Adapted from Exodus 14:5-9; 19-28

Brotherly Love

Beware. Your family may not always be your friends

"YOU CAN'T LET HIM GO out there!"

"Watch me."

"Are you crazy? That, that monster will destroy him."

"Let's see."

"Oh, come on, he hasn't got a prayer."

"Who knows? Maybe a prayer is exactly what he has."

"Man, that's our baby brother, going up against a nine-foot six-inch freak. Where's your heart?"

"Haven't you been listening? Our 'baby brother' killed a lion. And a bear. Over a few scraggly sheep. He's done it before. He can do it again."

"You think we don't know what this is about? You think we don't see through you?"

"What are you on about?"

"Stop pretending."

"Say it."

"You're still vexed because the prophet chose him over you! You honestly think anything happens to him the prophet's coming back to you?"

Eliab squared up to his younger brother, stung by his words. Shammah stood his ground.

"Go on then Eliab."

Abinadab, the second oldest brother, jumped in and forced them apart.

"Stop! We're brothers. That's our enemy out there, that Philistine."

"Yes," Shammah retorted. "And that's our baby brother out there because none of us has got the stones to go out there and take this freak on."

"Be my guest, Shammah." Shammah pressed towards Eliab but Abinadab held him back.

"Calm down the both of you! And anyway, it's too late. He's already out there."

They looked at their brother in the valley, as he knelt beside a brook.

"What's going on? What's he doing? Where's his armour?"

"He refused," replied Abinadab. "Said it's untested."

"No! No!" shouted Shammah, falling to the ground. Eliab flinched, for a moment wishing he had dragged his brother back from his insane quest. He was annoying, but he was still their baby brother. Their father would be heartbroken. But seeing him now running towards the giant his conscience fell silent again.

"If he really is the anointed one," he said, "he'll get through this."

And if not, he thought, then I guess I'll just have to prepare myself. The faint smile was almost imperceptible, but not quite. Shammah interrupted his thoughts as he faced him.

"I promise you this Eliab. If David dies at the hand of the giant, I will bury two brothers today."

They stood face to face, hands on swords. This time, Abinadab stepped back.

*Adapted from 1 Samuel 17:12-14; 29-48

I Saw You Last Night

Who is in charge? Who is calling the shots?

"MY KING."

Her voice ghosted across the room, bearing two small words weighted with promise. The king felt the words settle in his stomach, then spread throughout his entire body. A tremor surged through every extremity leaving a quiver in his chest. He fought to bring his response under regal control; he could not display any physical cues to his yearning. At least, not yet. How could he have expected that her voice carried the same impact as seeing her from afar earlier that evening?

The king dismissed the attendant who had brought her to him, then called for her to come close. The scent of perfumed spices as she approached set his already quickened pulse racing even faster. He stretched out his hand and raised her chin, a signal for her to remove her veil.

If the view from his balcony had caused passion to flame, what he was seeing up close fanned those passions into a raging fire. He never imagined she had more secrets to share. Nothing left to expose that his eyes had not feasted on. Yet standing here now, his full appreciation of her exquisite beauty soared tenfold. Full yet defined lips, straight nose, sculpted cheekbones. The merest hint of a whisper of a smile, not enough to be improper, but enough to intrigue. The king took her hand, a soft hand so delicate it must soon slip away.

Sight. Sound. Smell. Touch. Enough to make a man forget that he was king, or that she belonged to another. Only one sense remained. Her eyes held his as he guided her without words towards his inner chamber.

The next evening she stood in her own chamber, ready to bathe. Once again she was slow, deliberate, oozing sensuality. She moved with the grace of a lily caressed by a gentle breeze as she prepared her water and spices. When the bath was ready she approached her window and looked up and across at the king's balcony. Sure enough, he was there again, peering in as he had done the previous night.

Her gaze lingered for a moment. She pulled her final layer of clothing up over her head and held it just in front of her for what seemed an eternity, before letting it slide to the ground. She raised both hands to the back of her head, loosened her hair, then brushed it backwards, ensuring maximum exposure.

Unlike the previous night however, she stretched upwards, gave one last look to the palace before she closed her shutters. As she turned and stepped into her bath, a smile spread across her face, just as the previous night.

*Adapted from 2 Samuel 11:2-4

Together Forever

The Lord is a jealous God

IT WASN'T BEING IN HIS tent making love in broad daylight that was exciting. Neither was it the mysterious forbidden woman that he was with.

No, that wasn't the exciting part.

It was the defiance that set his lust ablaze. To break all the rules and not care. Rules about worshipping other gods? Broken. Rules about graven images? So what? Rules about taking exotic women from forbidden nations? Didn't matter. He even brought his woman, Cozbi, into his tent in front of the so-called leaders. He didn't care.

And now, knowing Moses stood just outside, his loins caught fire as he lay on top of her. They didn't even care about the noise, too engrossed scaling erotic heights. They were together and no one could do a thing about it. No one would ever tear them apart.

But Zimri never reckoned on Phinehas, grandson of Aaron. He never knew that his passion for this Midianite woman paled compared to that of Phinehas. Passion for the God of Abraham, Isaac, and Jacob.

Zimri did not appreciate the hours upon hours that Phinehas had spent listening to his grandfather's tales about Abraham and Lot. Isaac and the wells at Rehoboth. Jacob wrestling with Esau and with the angel of the Lord. If Zimri had realised how much Phinehas loved the story of Joseph, Potiphar's wife, the prison and the palace, he might have thought twice.

If Zimri had known of the zeal of Phinehas, he would never have smirked at Phinehas when he came into his tent. He would never have sneered at him while in the middle of his exertions. He would have hushed Cozbi when she raised her head, looked at Phinehas and laughed, and then threw herself further into the act.

If only Zimri had known who Phinehas was and how he felt, he would not have ignored the spear in his hand.

Phinehas looked down, saw their mockery, and decided not to separate them. If they were that desperate to be together, they could stay together. He came and stood over Zimri, and drove the spear through his back, through Cozbi's stomach, fastening it and them to the ground.

Zimri was right after all. No one was going to separate him from Cozbi.

*Adapted from Numbers 25:6-8; 14,15

It's A Split Decision

Wisdom is the principal thing

DODIE LAUNCHED HERSELF AT LILA, knocking her rival to the ground despite her rival's greater size. Her grip tightened around Lila's throat as she straddled her.

"Where's my son? Where's my son? You dog, what have you done with him?

Lila's shock gave way to rage. She grabbed Dodi by her hair with one hand and yanked her head backwards as she flipped her over onto her back. Grabbing the other side of her head Lila slammed Dodi's head onto the ground over and over until she started to lose consciousness. Lila got up to grab a nearby clay pitcher. Dodi looked up through hazy eyes to see her nemesis standing over her sneering, with the pitcher raised high over her head. As the pitcher came down, Dodi closed her eyes.

"Nooo!"

Lila crashed to the ground as her husband Uriyon knocked her clean off her feet. The pitcher splintered into a thousand pieces, sending shards of sharp clay across the entire room.

"Are you mad?" cried Uriyon. "Have you lost your senses? What is wrong with you?"

Dodi struggled to her feet, and lunged towards her still prone rival. Uriyon wrestled her to the ground and grabbed her by her jaw.

"Stop this right now!"

The more Dodi fought, the more Uriyon's grip tightened, until her anger subsided.

*** ***

"My Lord and king, I stand before you perplexed. My wives are in bitter dispute, which will tear our household apart if no resolution is found."

Solomon stared at the three adults before him, the one woman holding a newborn. He glanced to his mother Bathsheba sitting on his left, questioning her with his gaze. 'This cannot be,' he thought. 'No, it cannot be.' Benaiah, captain of Israel's army stood at Solomon's right hand. He perceived no immediate danger but was still as intrigued as his king.

Solomon invited the petitioners to state their case.

Lila's story

"My king, I stand here before you as the injured party. I have suffered the jealous spite of this woman Dodie for many years, ever since Uriyon took her as his second wife and brought her to our home. From the very first day she has been nothing but poisonous to me. Never in front of Uriyon, but whenever he would leave us, I have suffered terribly at her hands. It has grown worse over the years as it became clear the LORD of heaven had closed her womb, maybe in judgement of her bitter nature towards me and my three daughters.

"I have reached out to her as many times as the sun has risen in the east. I have offered to help her in her duties, I have advised her, I have held her hand as she lamented her judgement. I have lent my youngest to her for her to experience in some small way the beauty of motherhood. Each time she has bitten the hand reached out to her. I have come to the sad conclusion that the bitter waters of Mara flow from her very soul, but I could never have imagined this.

"By the great mercies of the LORD Almighty we both became with child within days of each other. Even then, despite her animosity, I tried to share with her the benefit of my experience but alas, to no avail. Then as the LORD would have it, we both bore a man child two nights past, she in her quarters, I in mine. A boy at last! I was so elated after what was a difficult childbirth that I did not even know at the time that she too had given birth."

Solomon shifted in his seat and gave Bathsheba another puzzled look, before beckoning Lila to continue.

"This morning as I suckled my son, I heard wailing coming from Dodie's quarters. I gathered immediately that her poor infant must have perished throughout the night. Perhaps in her keenness and inexperience she smothered the child whilst sleeping. The wailing soon turned from grief to bitterness. Moments later Dodie burst into my quarters with the most venomous of accusations, charging me that I had exchanged my son for hers. I barely had time to put my son down before she flung herself at me. The force of her small frame against me came with the ferocity of the returning waters of the Red Sea upon the Egyptian chariots. Had Uriyon not intervened I have no doubt I would now be as dead as her offspring.

"And now my king, I stand before you at your mercy. She claims that the child in my arms is hers. My lord, as a lion amongst men, gifted to know the hearts of simple women, I ask that you defend my cause."

Solomon leaned his head to one side, and turned to Bathsheba, scowling. "Tell me mother, what transpires? What madness is this? Is this some jest that the court has created?"

"My lord, I am as bemused as you are," Bathsheba replied.

Solomon beckoned to Dodie. "You. Come forward. Tell me your tale." Dodie stepped forward.

Dodie's story

"O great king Solomon, I have but few words. I cannot begin to describe how this woman and her three daughters have maligned me ever since I became wife to Uriyon. The tales would be too great to believe, my king. It is already a miracle that I am still alive to present my cause before you. But my lord, I know what it is to see miracles. For fourteen years the Lord has closed my womb. That was already a burden so great to bear, notwithstanding the terrible cruelty I endured from my enemy.

"My lord, last night I lay down with my son, it is true. After the LORD graciously and miraculously opened my womb, how could I so soon let him go. However, my labour took a great toll on my strength, causing my sleep to be deep.

"I awoke this morning to feel the lifeless child in my arms. I wept bitterly, clutching him to my chest. I confess my king that I charged the LORD with the greatest of cruelty. I asked him why He had treated me as Naomi, and changed my name to Bitterness. However, when I took time to gaze upon my son's features, another horror crept upon me: it was not my child. My horror grew darker as I realised what my jealous bitter rival had done. I also confess that when she denied what she had done, reason left me and I threw myself at her, caring not for my own life.

"Now my king, I have no strength left to fight, no strength for long tales, or for Lila's wickedness. My simple plea, O king, restore my child to me."

Solomon looked from one woman to the other.

"Daughters of Israel, tell me the truth. Is this not a jest? For not more than two hours ago, two women less noble than yourselves stood before me with almost the exact same tale. And now, you? Confess both, then go your way, no harm is done." All parties stood in silence, with somewhat bemused expressions on their collective faces.

"Uriyon, you are husband to both, and father of this child. Tell me, which of these is the true mother to the child before me?" Uriyon remained rooted to the spot, cheeks flushed.

"My…my king… I…I…I cannot say."

Solomon leaned forward. "Then tell me this. Of which of your wives are you more afraid?" The colour in Uriyon's cheeks deepened. "No matter," Solomon continued. "I will decide for you. Benaiah, hand me your sword."

"Daughters of Israel, the LORD God has today proven that He alone knows the secrets of human hearts, and that He alone is truly just and equitable. Lila, bring me the child. We will divide him in two that you may have an equal share."

Dodi watched in horror as Lila stepped forward with the child. Everything slowed. She tried to say something but nothing would come. Lila lay the baby at the king's feet. "So let it be done my Lord," she said.

Solomon turned to Uriyon. "Come Uriyon, I invite you to be a man in your own house. Take this sword and divide the child. You may still be father to both halves." Uriyon stood open mouthed, hand trembling as his knees shook.

"Still cannot lead your house, Uriyon? No matter, your king will help you."

Solomon rose from his throne and approached the child. Sweeping his robe behind him, he raised the sword in both hands. Dodi's own hands tore at her clothes as she watched, mouth gasping for air.

"For you Dodi! For you Lila!" The sword began its arc downwards.

"Noooo!" The shriek from Dodi rang through the throne room as she fell to her knees clutching her belly. "Let Lila have him. Let him be hers, let him live!" The clang of the sword striking the floor reverberated up through Dodi's chest.

*** ***

Lila watched through screwed eyes from her new quarters as Dodi sat in the courtyard rocking her son while Uriyon crouched in front of them making baby noises.

'It came from her own lips,' Lila thought. 'Let Lila have him! Let Lila have him!' And have him I will, they'll see. And if I do not have that boy, then as my soul lives, no one will.'

For the merest moment Dodi shuddered as an icy shadow passed over her soul.

*Inspired by 1 Samuel 1:1-6; 1 Kings 3:16-28

Men!

Do not fear evildoers; our God is not sleeping

THE QUEEN EXCELLED AT handling men. She murdered hundreds of prophets who spoke for the True God and instituted Baal worship. When the man of God killed over eight hundred of her prophets, she put out a death threat, causing him to flee and give up on life.

When she found the king lying in bed and refusing to eat over a vineyard, she took charge. No matter that the vineyard was a family legacy belonging to his neighbour. She set the owner up on false charges, got him executed, and got her husband the land he wanted.

Weeks later the notorious king slayer Jehu turned up at her gate. Although he had been on a killing spree she wasn't threatened in the slightest. Why would she be? Jehu was another man, and she knew how to handle men. She put on her makeup and fixed up her hair, then looked out of her third-storey window. She returned his glare, refusing to be intimidated, and started to taunt him.

"Who is with me?" Jehu shouted as he scanned the upper windows. "Who?" The Queen's servants appeared at one window.

"Throw her down!"

As the men approached her, the Queen remained unconcerned. They're men, she reasoned. Easy to manipulate, to control. Find their emotional weakness. Fear, depression, lust, they all had one. Especially lust. When you find their weakness, squeeze. Predict their responses, dictate their actions.

Her servants grabbed her and threw her through the window. Blood splattered up the wall as she landed. When they came to retrieve the body, they found nothing but her skull, the palms of her hands, and her feet. A prophet had warned the king that in the place that dogs licked Naboth's blood, the same would happen to them. But, in her case, these dogs were hungry.

Poor Queen Jezebel. She could handle men, yet her male servants betrayed her. It was as she went through the window to her death, she realised her fatal error. Her servants were all eunuchs.

*Adapted from 2 Kings 9:20-37

Withdrawn

The sex was great. The afterglow? Not so good

ENTWINED, THEIR BODIES MOVE as one. This isn't a fight but they are on the edge of violent, primal heat set to full. Neither one wants this to stop. They are doing their duty, obeying orders, and loving every minute.

This started as an embarrassment for her, then became a chore. But now the shackles are off. Why just endure, why not enjoy? The Woman has let her desires off the leash and she refuses to be quiet and polite. Desire is not demure, it is voracious and demanding, devouring and unashamed. Her last reservation had disappeared the moment his hand stroked her shoulder. Her husband may have died but her passion had survived. And now, her passion is alive in a way it's never been. But, doing this with his brother? Who cares. Her eyes close.

The Man is losing it. He was in control, had it worked out. Nobody and nothing would tell him what to do. No father, nor antiquated custom. He has chosen of his own will to comply, but it will be on his terms. He alone will define how this ends. His mind has worked out a plan on how to have the pleasure but not the consequence. Earlier he had reflected on his deceased older brother and smiled to himself. When he was young he tried on his brother's clothes, his brother's sandals. Why not his brother's wife?

But now forget the plan. Now he's losing it. Desire is rising from his toes, up his shins and calves and thighs, and further. From his chest, through his abdomen, it converges, gathered for the grand release. He wants to delay but release, prolong but finish. His eyes close.

'This will be your brother's seed.'

The words crash into his head and snap him back into line. All this to honour his dead brother, the firstborn? Any child born will not be his, nor bear his name. Well not today brother.

The passion is heading towards the climax, moving through the corridor, ready to break out.

'This will be your brother's seed.'

He rips his body off hers, rolling over onto his back and straight onto his side. At once, the passion hits the open air, and life shoots out, crashing onto the ground. The Woman groans, unfulfilled and in despair, but alas too late. Life-bearing fluid continues to crash to the ground, wave after compelling wave mingling with the dust.

'So much for my brother's seed.' In his head he celebrates victory, his twisted grin a chequered flag.

'Your brother's seed.' This time the voice inside his head is not his.

'Your brother's seed.' The Man's head throbs as the voice booms.

'Your brother's seed.' Another spasm, but this time in his chest. His arms tingle while his chest tightens. His head and heart pounds, as he rasps for breath.

One last time the voice screams.

'Your Brother's Seed!'

His heart crashes, his mind shuts down forever as he lies on his side. He draws his last breath, eyes wide open.

*Adapted from Genesis 38:8-10

It's Not The Fall, It's The Landing That Kills

If sin continues, don't expect a happy ending

FOR ELI THE WAITING WAS the worst. News of the state of the battle was slow in reaching the home front. The last information they received wasn't good. The Philistines were pressing hard and Israel was being pushed back.

Whenever the nation lost a battle in the past, it was a sign they had backslidden. Eli recalled the battle at Ai, one Israel should have won with ease. Instead, the enemy humiliated them because of the sin of one man.

If one man's sin caused such humiliation, what of two? What of his sons Hophni and Phineas? He grieved as he considered the path these young men had taken. Stories were coming out about them fornicating at the doors of the tabernacle. Even worse, they stole from the people's sacrifices, causing them to blaspheme.

Eli had pleaded with them more than once. In his heart he knew he should have removed them.

"The Ark," cried the messenger. "They've sent for the Ark."

Eli's mind scrambled. If the army sent for the Ark of the Covenant, the battle must be desperate. How many lives have we lost? How close are the enemy? Are we in danger of destruction? Again? For years Israel's disobedience had resulted in judgement by other nations, which only ended when God raised up judges such as Deborah, Gideon, Jephthah and the mighty Samson. Eli was the latest in line, but he had nothing to offer on the battlefield. The only thing he could do was hope his sons redeem themselves and make their lives worthwhile.

"My sons, go with the Ark. Let it not rest on the ground nor go out of your sight. Defend it with your lives, for on the Ark hangs the future of Israel. It is better I lose two sons, than our people lose the Glory between the Cherubims. I can live childless. Israel cannot live without the Lord."

"Be still my father," said Phinehas. "Although you count our lives for nothing, we will go with this token, and when we prevail, we will come again and restore your precious treasure. And Israel will praise the names of Phinehas and Hophni, saviours of the nation."

With that, Phineas wheeled away and led the procession towards the camp. Behind him, Hophni glared at his father, while his mind raged at his father's disregard for their lives. He vowed to himself that on their return, Eli's tenure would end. He too wheeled aside and rode after his brother.

Eli sat back on the wall near the tabernacle. Those who waited with him, unable to fight, saw the troubled look on his face. This was a time for celebration. How could Israel succumb when Elohim's holy presence went in front? Still, the sense of foreboding did not go away. A dark cloud rested over his spirit. It was not possible that Israel fall, that the enemy extinguish the light of the people, and the Ark meet with harm. Not when El-Elyon, the one who created the heavens and the earth, was with them. Surely not. Yet the cloud remained.

Even from miles away, those remaining at Shiloh heard the shout carried by the wind from Ebenezer where the army camped. Phinehas and Hophni rode into camp accompanied by the Most High. They rallied the troops and assured them of the coming victory. The roar crossed the valley to Aphek where the Philistines had gathered. Even they knew what the sound meant.

The sound that carried back to Shiloh lifted Eli's spirits. He lifted his face to the heavens to bless the Lord for sparing his people another day. Judgement had given way to mercy.

It was just before the ninth hour when the messenger returned and fell at Eli's feet.

"Master, your sons fought with valour. Each of them slew dozens of the Philistine army as men born for war. Their swords drank the blood of the heathen, separating heads from shoulders, creating widows and orphans. The day will come when the women of Israel will celebrate their deeds in song. Tales will echo of the legend of these warriors who met the battle with bravery right to the end."

Eli's heart trembled.

"End? What do you mean by the end? Where are my sons, where is the Ark?"

"Alas, my master, your sons Phinehas and Hophni are dead. They died as heroes."

"And the Ark, what of the Ark?"

"The Ark has fallen, taken captive by the enemy."

Blood drained from Eli's face as his head spun. His limbs became lifeless, unable to steady his heavy frame. The wall he fell from was thirty inches from the ground. If he had not landed on his neck, he may have survived. With the Ark of the Covenant lost, and the Glory of Israel removed, it was better this way.

*Adapted from 1 Samuel 4:1-18

For Crying Out Loud

What you sow today may impact a generation tomorrow

I CAN'T BELIEVE YOU JUST DID that to me.

I could tell yesterday from your face you were upset. You tried to keep it straight, no emotion. But your actions were off. Even when you said it was okay, the tone said otherwise. And you wouldn't look me in the face, in the eye. At home, you never said a word to me. Even Mom and Dad asked me, and I said nothing.

I was glad when I saw you coming. I followed you, hoping we would straighten things out. But your eyes gave you away. And even when I begged you to stop hitting me with that rock you kept going, again and again, as if something had possessed you.

I can't believe it. My twin brother! Do you realise what you've done though? Do you know what you've started?

More brothers will kill each other. Sisters will kill each other. Husbands killing wives, wives killing husbands.

Complete strangers will kill each other, families turn on one another. Time will come when you can't go anywhere without hearing that people are killing each other.

People won't go out without wondering if they will come back home. Or their family. A man will kill someone because he thinks the person will kill him.

They will invent different ways to kill. Some will use their hands as you did. Keep hitting each other or putting their hands round each other's throats and squeeze. Others will use tools. The tools will get bigger. Big enough to kill families, groups, masses at the same time. It will get to where people invent and invest in new ways to kill.

People won't talk and reason anymore, they'll just kill. If they wanted, they could sit around a table, talk things through, work things out. That's what I wanted to do with you. I wanted to talk about why my offering was accepted and yours rejected. Thing is, He didn't reject you, just your offering. You could have made another one, a better one, and He would have accepted it too, but no, you had to make it personal.

You had to blame someone, anyone but yourself. So you blamed me. It's not as if it was my fault, I just gave the best of what I had and thought you had done the same, how was I supposed to know? I used to think of you as my protector, my keeper. But I guess I was wrong.

You know what though brother? I loved you, but I'm not taking this. Oh, you think because I'm dead it's finished? No brother. Trust me, I will be in your head from now on. Anywhere you go I'll be there. While you are walking, running, resting, I'll be there. Whoever you're with I'll be there, and I will make sure everybody knows what you've done. And when you're on your own, oh boy!

I demand justice; I demand vengeance. Only animals should shed their blood. Not people. Not twin brothers. It's done now, but it's not over, brother. I am prepared to cry out to our Maker. Cry out until He hears me, and I won't stop until He avenges me. Brother, you don't realise what you have just done.

*Adapted from Genesis 4:1-10

THE END

About the Author

I HAVE BEEN A PART OF the church all my life, as the church has been a part of me. I have been formally involved in the ministry for over thirty years. I currently serve as the pastor of Zion City Tabernacle in Wolverhampton, West Midlands, since it started in November 2008.

My ministry gifts primarily encompass exhortation and teaching. I have had the privilege of sharing these throughout the U.K., and parts of North America, and the Caribbean.

I have been happily married since 1986, and have three grown children. I also work part time as a civil servant.

Favourite authors right now are J.F. Penn and Alana Terry.

Books by the Author

NON-FICTION

A Time To Speak Out: The Bible, The Church, and Victims of Domestic Violence and Abuse
Print: ISBN 978-0-9935226-1-1
eBook: ISBN 978-0-9935226-0-4

When A Man Says I Will This Is What It Means
eBook: ISBN 978-0-9935226-4-2

When A Man Says I Will This Is What It Means Workbook
Print: ISBN 978-0-9935226-6-6

When A Woman Says I Will This Is What It Means
eBook: ISBN 978-0-9935226-5-9

When A Woman Says I Will This Is What It Means Workbook
Print: ISBN 978-0-9935226-7-3

FICTION

Free: My Abuse Is Over
Print: ISBN 978-0-9935226-3-5
eBook: ISBN 978-0-9935226-2-8

Why God? A Dream. A Fantasy. A Nightmare
eBook only: ISBN 978-0-9935226-8-0

All available from your favourite online bookstore

Thank you for reading
DARK: BIBLE STORIES FOR ADULTS
I hope you enjoyed it. Please leave a review from wherever you ordered this book

Thank you to my family for your patience and support

Thank you to my friends for your encouragement

As ever, all praise to the Lord Jesus Christ

Printed in Great Britain
by Amazon

74781049R00076